PHILIP PROWSE

L. A. Winners

MACMILLAN READERS
ELEMENTARY LEVEL

Founding Editor: John Milne

The Macmillan Readers provide a choice of enjoyable reading materials for learners of English. The series is published at six levels – Starter, Beginner, Elementary, Pre-intermediate, Intermediate and Upper.

Level control

Information, structure and vocabulary are controlled to suit the students' ability at each level.

The number of words at each level:

Starter	about 300 basic words
Beginner	about 600 basic words
Elementary	about 1100 basic words
Pre-intermediate	about 1400 basic words
Intermediate	about 1600 basic words
Upper	about 2200 basic words

Vocabulary

Some difficult words and phrases in this book are important for understanding the story. Some of these words are explained in the story and some are shown in the pictures. From Pre-intermediate level upwards, words are marked with a number like this: ...³. These words are explained in the Glossary at the end of the book.

Contents

California Dreaming

I was dreaming about Hawaii. I was dreaming about my holiday. In my dream, I was on the beach in Hawaii. The hot sun was shining on my face. The sound of the sea was all around me.

But it *was* a dream. Three weeks ago, I *had* been lying on a beach in Hawaii. But I was not in Hawaii now. I was dreaming in my office in Los Angeles. I had returned from my holiday and there was no work for me. Nobody wanted to hire me. I went to my office every day, but the telephone didn't ring. So I slept in my chair and I dreamt about Hawaii.

I was dreaming a wonderful dream. The sun was hot. The noise of the sea was loud and there was a beautiful woman standing next to me.

Suddenly, there was a voice in my dream. Somebody was calling my name.

'Mr Samuel! Mr Samuel, wake up! Please, wake up! I want to talk to you.'

I opened my eyes. It was April in Los Angeles. The hot sun was shining on my face. The sun was shining through my office window. And there was a woman standing beside me. She was calling my name. But she was angry with me.

'Mr Samuel. Wake up! Why are you sleeping at 11.45 in the morning?'

The woman was about twenty-five years old. She had long dark hair. She was wearing a short green dress and a brown leather coat. She had a lovely face.

'Perhaps this woman is a client,' I thought. 'Perhaps she'll hire me. Perhaps she has a job for me.'

I smiled at the woman. But she did not smile at me.

'Are you Lenny Samuel, the private detective?' she asked.

'Yes, I'm Lenny,' I said. 'Please sit down.' I pointed to a wooden chair on the other side of my desk.

The woman looked around my office. She looked at

5

the old furniture and the dirty windows. She looked at the broken blind and the plastic coffee cups in the waste bin. Then she looked at me. I hadn't shaved. And my suit and hair were untidy. The woman didn't speak.

Suddenly, she took a handkerchief out of her bag. She wiped the dust from the chair and she sat down.

'Mr Samuel,' she said. 'I saw your name and address in the telephone book. Are you cheap? And are you a good detective?'

'I'm not *good*,' I replied. 'I'm the *best*. The best private detective in L.A.'

The woman laughed. 'Are you joking?' she said. 'The best private detectives have secretaries. And the best private detectives don't have dirty, untidy offices. But I want to hire you. Will you do a job for me, Mr Samuel?'

'What do you want me to do?' I asked.

I didn't like the woman. She was rude. But I needed money. I needed money quickly. My holiday in Hawaii had cost $1000. I had borrowed the money. Now I had to pay back the money.

I hadn't borrowed $1000 from a bank. I had borrowed it from Herman. Herman was a bodyguard. His office was next to mine. He worked for film stars. He was very tall – more than two metres – and he weighed one hundred and forty kilos. Now Herman wanted his money back. And when Herman wanted something, he always got it.

I smiled at the woman again.

She didn't smile at me. She got up from her chair and walked to the window. My office is on the fourth floor of an old building.

The woman looked down at the street. Then she turned round.

'Mr Samuel, I want you to find The Chief,' she said. 'He disappeared yesterday morning. Something has happened to him – something bad.'

'OK,' I said. I took a notepad and a pen out of my desk. 'Describe him, please. But I must tell you something. I'll do almost any work. But there is one thing that I won't do. I won't look for husbands who have disappeared. Is The Chief your husband?'

'No,' the woman said. 'The Chief isn't my husband. The Chief is a horse!'

2

Sandy Bonner

I looked at the woman in the green dress.

'A horse?' I said. 'You want me to find a horse?' Was the woman joking?

'Yes,' she replied. 'I want you to find a horse.'

'Miss,' I said. 'I don't know anything about horses. Horses have four legs and they run around. I don't know anything more about them.'

'OK, now you'll learn more about horses, Mr Samuel,' the woman said.

There was a noise outside my door. The woman turned and looked at it. Suddenly, she was frightened.

Somebody knocked at the door. It was a glass door. The words L. SAMUEL – PRIVATE INVESTIGATOR were written on it in big black letters.

The person who was outside the door knocked again. He knocked very hard.

'Come in!' I shouted. 'Don't break the glass!'

The door opened and a huge man walked in. He was very tall – more than two metres – and he weighed one hundred and forty kilos. It was Herman.

'Hi, Lenny,' Herman said. 'I've come for my money. Have you got it?'

Then Herman saw the dark-haired woman sitting by the desk. He smiled at her. Herman had lots of white teeth.

'Oh, I'm sorry, miss,' he said. 'I didn't see you when I came in. Are you talking about business with Lenny? I'll come back later.'

Herman smiled at the woman again. Then he turned and left the room.

'Who's that?' the woman asked. She wasn't frightened now. 'He's big and strong. Perhaps he'll help me to find my horse.'

'No! No, he won't,' I replied quickly. 'That was Herman. He's a bodyguard. He's not a detective. *I* can find the horse that you've lost.'

'But I haven't *lost* the horse,' the woman said. 'People don't *lose* horses, Mr Samuel. Horses run away or —'

'Or someone steals them?' I asked.

'Yes,' she replied.

'OK,' I said. 'Tell me the facts. Describe the horse, please.'

'He's twelve years old and two metres high. He has brown hair and brown eyes,' she replied.

'I'm sorry,' I said. 'That description won't help me. Have you got a photograph of him?'

The woman smiled. 'Yes,' she said. 'Here's a photo of The Chief. The picture was taken after his last race.'

'I'll come back later,' said Herman.

'The Chief is a racehorse?' I asked.

'He *was* a racehorse,' she replied. 'He was one of the best racehorses.'

The woman gave me a colour photo. It was a picture from a magazine. It was a picture of a big brown horse. It was standing by a crowd of people. Some of the people were touching the horse. Next to it, there was a jockey in brightly-coloured riding clothes.

'That's The Chief,' the woman said. 'The photo was taken at Hollywood Park Racetrack, two years ago. It was taken when The Chief won an important race.'

'Wow!' I said. I didn't know anything about horse-racing. But Hollywood Park Racetrack is a very well-known racetrack.

'So the horse is a racehorse called The Chief,' I said.

'No. I told you,' the woman said. 'The Chief *was* a racehorse. He doesn't race now. The Chief lives with me at my ranch now. He has retired from racing.'

'So you have a ranch?' I asked.

I thought about the job. 'This woman has a ranch,' I thought. 'So she has a lot of money. If I work for her for five days, I'll earn $1000. I'll be able to pay Herman.'

'Yes, I have a ranch,' the woman replied. 'It's called the Ride-A-Winner Ranch. It's in the hills. It's near the Santa Rosita Racetrack.'

I wrote these facts on my notepad. I knew about Santa Rosita. It was a small racetrack, but it was very popular.

'I keep retired racehorses – horses that don't race any more,' the woman said. 'People come and stay at the ranch. And —'

'And they ride the horses,' I said. 'And your name is?'

'My name is Sandy Bonner,' she said.

'What's your phone number?' I asked.

'You mustn't phone me. I'll phone *you*,' she said quickly. 'And you mustn't come to the ranch.'

'Why mustn't I come to the ranch, Miss Bonner?' I asked.

'Mr Samuel,' Sandy Bonner replied, 'you are working for me. I'm going to pay you. You mustn't ask me any more questions. How much money do you want?'

'I want $200 a day,' I said.

Sandy Bonner took some banknotes from her bag and she gave them to me.

'OK, Mr Samuel. Here's $200,' she said. 'I'll phone you this evening.'

She stood up and walked to the door.

'Wait a minute, Sandy,' I said quickly. 'I need to know more facts. When did The Chief disappear? And *how* did he disappear?'

Sandy turned and she looked at me.

'He disappeared yesterday morning,' she replied. 'A man came to the ranch. He wanted to ride The Chief. He paid $100 to ride the horse for an hour.'

'Wow!' I thought. 'I'm in the wrong business! I earn $200 a day. This horse earns $100 an hour!'

'The man paid me and he rode away on The Chief,' Sandy went on. 'That was at ten o'clock. The man didn't come back and neither did the horse.'

'Did this man ride away alone?' I asked.

'Yes,' Sandy said. 'I usually ride with visitors but I was busy yesterday. The man was a good rider. I wasn't worried.'

'Did you know the man who took the horse?' I asked.

'I'd never seen him before,' she replied. 'But he told

me his name. He was called Dick Gates.'

'Did Mr Gates show you any ID? Any identification papers?' I asked.

Sandy shook her head. 'No, Mr Samuel,' she said.

'So a stranger rode away on a valuable horse,' I said. 'And he didn't come back. Were you surprised?'

'Yes, I was surprised,' Sandy said quietly. 'Mr Gates gave me a phone number. But when I phoned the number, there was no reply.'

'Did you call the police?' I asked.

'No ... no, I didn't,' Sandy replied slowly. Then she stopped speaking. She was very worried. She walked back to the chair and she sat down again.

'Why didn't you call the police, Sandy?' I asked.

'Because I got a phone call,' Sandy answered. 'Two hours after Dick Gates rode away on The Chief, a man phoned me,' she said. 'I don't know who the man was. He wasn't Gates. The man said, "I've got The Chief, Miss Bonner. I've borrowed the horse. I'll return him after a few days. But if you call the police, The Chief will be killed. We're watching you." So I don't want you to phone me, Mr Samuel. And I don't want you to come to the ranch. If you do, these men will kill The Chief.'

'OK,' I said. 'I understand. Describe Mr Gates, please.'

'He was about forty years old. And he was tall and heavy,' said Sandy. 'He had long red hair. It was tied in a pony-tail. He was wearing blue jeans and a brown jacket.'

'That's a very good description,' I said. 'Did he come to the ranch in a car?'

'I don't know,' Sandy said. She looked at her watch. 'I have to go now. I'll phone you this evening.'

She stood up and she walked to the window. She

looked down at the street for half a minute. Then she walked to the door.

'Goodbye, Mr Samuel. Please find The Chief for me,' she said.

3

The Ride-A-Winner Ranch

I watched Sandy Bonner leave my office. She had told me a very strange story. Was her story true? I wanted to find out about her. I decided to follow her.

I picked up my hat and my jacket. Quickly, I left the office.

I ran down the stairs. When I got to the hallway, Sandy had left the building. I went outside. I saw Sandy at the corner of the street. She was getting into a small black car – a 4x4. I got into my own car, which was parked near the office building.

As Sandy drove away, I started my old grey Chrysler and I joined the traffic. Sandy Bonner's black 4x4 was a hundred metres in front of me.

It was a beautiful Friday in L.A. Blue sky, sunshine and smog! There was a lot of traffic. The engines of the cars, trucks and buses made the smog in the air. I thought about the clean air in Hawaii. Then I thought about Herman and about the money that I owed him.

The traffic moved slowly. There were four cars between me and the black 4x4. Sandy drove through the city and then towards Pasadena. I followed her. We turned onto the Foothills Freeway. We drove east, towards the San Gabriel Mountains.

Forty-five minutes later, I was driving past the Santa Rosita Racetrack. Sandy was still a hundred metres in front of me. But after another ten minutes, the black 4x4 turned off the freeway. I turned off too, and I started to follow Sandy's car along a small road. But I slowed down. Soon, I was about three hundred metres behind Sandy. I didn't want her to see me.

The road was straight and flat. There were dry bushes on each side of the road and there was dry grass. The grass was yellow and dusty. After about three kilometres, I saw some trees. The black 4x4 turned off the road near the trees. Sandy drove onto a track. I slowed down again and I stopped the Chrysler.

I watched Sandy's car. The 4x4 went along the track for three hundred metres. Then it stopped near some buildings. Sandy got out of the car and she went into one of the buildings.

I started the Chrysler again and I drove slowly towards the trees. I turned off the road and onto the track. Where the track joined the road, there was a red and white sign. The words RIDE-A-WINNER RANCH were painted on it. After a few metres, I turned off the track and I parked the car in the trees.

There was a pair of binoculars in the Chrysler. I picked them up and got out of the car. I leant on the top of the car and I pointed the binoculars at the buildings.

I looked through the binoculars. I saw a large white ranch house. And I saw some long, low, wooden buildings next to it. There were some horses near these buildings.

'The low buildings are the stables where the horses are kept,' I said to myself.

I got back into the car and I waited. I could see the

ranch but no one at the ranch could see me or the Chrysler.

Half an hour later, a car came along the road and turned onto the track. The car passed me and it went towards the ranch house. It was a big red 4x4.

The red 4x4 stopped next to Sandy's black car and a man got out. He went into the ranch house. I sat in my car and waited. Nothing moved. It was hot and dusty. No one was riding a horse. Nothing happened.

I decided to go closer to the ranch house. I looked at the track between the trees and the ranch house. There were some bushes at the side of the track. The bushes were half-way between the house and my car. I got out of the Chrysler.

I ran, with the binoculars in one hand, towards the bushes. When I reached the bushes, I lay down on the ground. The ground was hot and very dusty. I lifted the binoculars and I looked through them.

I could see the ranch house clearly now. I could see the red and black cars outside. The red 4x4 was turned towards me. There was a piece of paper fixed to its front window. I turned a small wheel on my binoculars. Now I could see the paper more clearly. I read some words on the paper. The paper was a car-park ticket for the Santa Rosita Racetrack.

Then I turned the wheel on my binoculars again. I looked at the house. Immediately, I saw Sandy Bonner. She was inside the house. She was standing near one of the large windows. She was talking to someone – a tall, slim man with dark hair.

'That man isn't Dick Gates,' I thought. 'Gates has red hair.'

15

Suddenly, Sandy stepped forward and hit the man across the face. The man lifted his hand. Was he going to hit Sandy? At that moment, Sandy moved away from the window. I couldn't see what happened next.

I stood up. I was going to run to the ranch house and help Sandy.

'Stay where you are!' a man shouted.

I turned. About five metres behind me, there was an old man. He was wearing blue overalls, a cotton shirt and a wide hat. He had a rifle in his hands. He was pointing the gun at me.

I smiled and I started to walk towards the old man.

'Hi!' I said. 'What's wrong?'

There was a shot from the rifle and the dust by my feet flew into the air. I stopped.

'Who are you, stranger?' the old man asked. 'What are you doing here?'

I thought for a few seconds. The old man chewed gum slowly. He watched me.

'I – I'm watching birds,' I said, smiling. I showed him my binoculars. 'There were some interesting birds over there.' I pointed towards the house. 'I was watching them.'

The old man looked towards the ranch house.

'There aren't any birds there, mister,' he said.

I smiled again. 'No, there aren't,' I said. 'When you fired your rifle, you frightened the birds.'

'People don't wear suits when they watch birds,' the old man said angrily. 'Why are you hiding in these bushes? This is private land. Now go back to your car and leave.' The old man stepped forward and pushed me with the rifle.

16

'Who are you, stranger?' the old man asked.

'Who are *you*?' I asked. 'And why are you telling me what to do?'

'I'm Lou Weaver. I work here. I've worked for Miss Bonner's family for more than thirty years,' the old man said. He pushed me with the rifle again. 'Miss Bonner is my boss. I do what she tells me to do. I have this gun and I'm telling you what to do. Now leave – and stay away from here.'

I turned and walked quickly back to the Chrysler. I didn't say anything. I didn't tell the old man about my meeting with Sandy. Sandy Bonner had told me not to come to the ranch. I had made a mistake. I didn't want the old man to tell Sandy about my mistake.

Lou Weaver followed me. He stood in the trees as I got into the Chrysler. I saw him in the driving mirror as I drove away. Lou Weaver was chewing his gum and looking at me.

I drove back towards L.A. I had to help Sandy and I had to find The Chief. How? Then I remembered the car-park ticket on the window of the red 4x4. The words SANTA ROSITA RACETRACK were written on that car-park ticket. I didn't know anything about horse racing and racehorses. So I decided to go to Santa Rosita Racetrack. I wanted to find out about horse racing. And I wanted to find out more about the thin dark man. Perhaps someone at Santa Rosita knew him.

4

Santa Rosita Racetrack

I turned off the freeway at Santa Rosita Racetrack. It was a small racetrack but it was beautiful. There were tall trees by the dusty track. There were high, dark-blue mountains behind it. Some jockeys were riding their horses on the track. The sun shone down from the blue sky. It was late afternoon, but the sun was very bright. Everything was peaceful.

There weren't many cars in the car park. I parked my car and I put on a baseball cap and some dark glasses. Then I left the Chrysler and walked towards the track. I stood by the dusty track and watched the horses. There was no racing today. These horses were training.

The horses were very large and very fast. I was surprised. When a horse went past me, the noise from its feet was loud and dust flew into the air.

I looked around me. Near the track, there were some office buildings and some stables. There was a high fence around these buildings. I walked towards the stables area.

There was a gateway in the fence. The gate was very tall. It was closed. As I went nearer, I saw the gate open. A truck with a trailer came out. I didn't see anyone near the gate, but it closed behind the trailer.

I waited and watched. A few minutes passed. Then a 4x4 with a trailer came in from the road. The car stopped by the gate. There was a car-park ticket on the front window of the 4x4.

The driver put his head out of the side window of the car. He spoke into a metal box near the fence. Then the gate opened and the car and the trailer went through the gateway.

I walked over to the gate and I waited. A minute later, another car came in from the road. The driver spoke into the box. The gate opened. As the car went through the gateway, I walked beside it. Now I was inside the stables area. I walked a few metres away from the gateway.

'Hey, you!' a man shouted. Suddenly, someone came up behind me. He held my arms and pushed me against a stable wall.

'Stand against the wall! Hold your arms out! Don't turn round!' the man said.

I did what the man told me. He searched the pockets of my clothes. The man was behind me and I couldn't see his face. He took my detective's licence out of my pocket. Then there was a loud laugh. The man pulled off my baseball cap and my dark glasses.

'Lenny Samuel!' the man said. 'Turn round!'

I turned round. A big man was standing in front of me. He was wearing a brown uniform with a dark cap and glasses. I knew him. His name was Slim Peters. But his name was a joke. He wasn't thin – he was fat! Many years ago, both Slim and I had been L.A. policemen.

'Slim!' I said. 'What are you doing here?'

Slim pointed at his uniform. 'I'm a racetrack security guard,' he replied. 'But I'm asking *you* a question. What are *you* doing here?'

I didn't answer his question.

'How did you see me?' I asked.

Slim pointed to the gateway. 'I saw you on TV,' he replied. He laughed again.

There was a TV camera on the fence above the gate.

'Stand against the wall! Hold your arms out!
Don't turn round!' the man said.

Then Slim pointed to a small building near the gateway.

'I work over there,' he said.

'So you can see everyone who enters and leaves on TV?' I asked.

'Yes,' Slim replied. 'But Lenny, you haven't answered my question. What are *you* doing here?'

'I want to talk to someone who knows about racehorses, Slim,' I said. 'What happens to the best racehorses when they retire? Can you help me?'

I didn't ask Slim about the thin dark man who drove a red 4x4.

'Come to my office,' said Slim. 'We'll have some coffee. And we'll talk about your problem.'

We went to Slim's office and we sat down. Slim gave me back my detective's licence.

'Are you the only security guard here, Slim?' I asked.

'I'm the only guard here this afternoon,' Slim replied. 'There's no racing today. Friday is a training day. The horses are training today. Security is low on training days. There are more guards on racing days. When there's racing, security is very high. On racing days, we have to check everyone's ID. And the racetrack officials have to check the horses' IDs on racing days.'

'Do horses have ID?' I asked.

'Yes,' Slim replied. 'Every racehorse has a passport with a photograph and all the horse's details written in it. And every horse has a number tattooed inside its mouth.'

Slim made some coffee. We sat at his desk and drank the coffee. Slim looked at the TV screen as cars went in and out of the gate. Then we talked about my problem.

'Who shall I talk to about retired racehorses?' I asked Slim.

'Talk to the racehorse trainers who are here today,' Slim said. 'Ask one of the trainers about retired racehorses. But if you are going into the stables area, you must have a security pass. I'll give you one.'

He opened a drawer in his desk and he pulled out a pass. It was a small yellow card on a piece of cord. The words ALL AREAS were written on the card. Slim gave me the pass.

'You can use this today,' Slim said. 'Put it round your neck.'

'Can I use it tomorrow?' I asked.

'No. You can't use it tomorrow,' Slim replied. 'There are yellow passes for training days and blue passes for racing days. I can't give you a blue pass. Only racetrack officials, owners, trainers, jockeys and the people who take care of the horses have blue passes. Other people can't go into the stables area on racing days.'

I took the pass, but I continued talking to Slim. I learnt a lot about racetrack security. There was racing at Santa Rosita Racetrack from December to April. There were races on Wednesdays and Saturdays. Horses trained at the racetrack on the other days.

The horses' owners had stables at the racetrack. Horses were brought to the racetrack to train. They stayed in the stables while they were waiting to train. And they rested in the stables after training. Then the horses were taken away. On training days, trailers with horses were arriving and leaving all day. Nobody checked the horses or the trailers on training days.

On racing days, the horses stayed in the stables while they were waiting to race. And they rested in the stables after their races. But on racing days, the horses' IDs were checked carefully. The IDs were checked when the horses arrived at the racetrack. And they were checked again when they left. Racetrack officials looked at the horses' passports and at their tattoos.

After thirty minutes, I stood up and walked to the door. Slim had given me a lot of information. I tried to remember everything that he had told me.

'Thank you for your help,' I said to Slim. 'I'll talk to some trainers now.' I put the yellow security pass round my neck.

'OK, Lenny,' Slim said. 'I was pleased to help. Give me back the pass when you leave. Come here and watch the races tomorrow afternoon!'

I smiled. 'No, thank you,' I said, 'I'll be working.'

———

A few minutes later, I was watching some jockeys bringing their horses back to the stables. I talked to one of them. Then I talked to some of the people who took care of the horses. I found out some interesting facts about racing.

'People earn a lot of money from horse racing,' one woman told me. 'People bet millions of dollars on horse-races. The best racehorses are very valuable.

'Most racehorses are less valuable when they retire,' she went on. 'But some retired racehorses are used for breeding. Their owners breed young racehorses from them. These breeding horses are very valuable.'

None of this information helped me. Sandy didn't use The Chief for breeding. The Chief earned money because people wanted to ride a famous winner. The Chief was Sandy's horse. People who wanted to ride him knew that. Only Sandy could use the horse to earn money. So who

A few minutes later, I was watching some jockeys bringing their horses back to the stables.

had taken The Chief? And who was the thin dark man at the ranch? I decided to look for the red 4x4.

5

The Red 4x4

The doors of some of the stable buildings were open. I went into the buildings and I looked around. Some of the stables were quite small – they had stalls for only two horses. But some stables were large – they had stalls for five or more horses. Many of the stables were locked. I looked into some of them through their windows. Every stable had a number.

I watched two men bring a horse from a small stable – Stable 32. They put the horse into a trailer and they drove away. The stables area was quite busy and nobody looked at me. It was now early evening. Many horses were coming back from training on the track. Their jockeys took them to the stables to rest.

I walked along the roads between the stables.

'I'm not going to find The Chief here,' I thought. 'And I'm not going to learn anything more here. I need to talk to Sandy Bonner again. I'll go back to L.A. now. Sandy will phone me this evening.'

Suddenly, I saw a red 4x4 with a trailer. It was near a large stable – Stable 14 – which was a hundred metres from me. A tall, slim, dark man was shutting the stable doors.

'Is that the 4x4 that I saw at Sandy's ranch?' I asked myself. 'I don't know. There are hundreds of red 4x4s in

L.A. And there are thousands of tall, slim, dark men.'

A minute later, the red 4x4 went past me. It was going towards the gateway. There were two people in the car. As the car passed me, I saw the driver's face. He *was* the tall slim man that I had seen at Sandy's ranch. He was the man that Sandy had hit. I couldn't see the other person clearly. Was it a man or a woman? I didn't know.

I watched the car. It stopped at the gate for a moment and then it left the stables area. I walked towards Stable 14. There was no one near the building. The doors were closed. I went to the side of the building and tried to look through the window. But I couldn't see into the stable. There was some wood fixed inside the window.

I put my hand in my pocket and I took out my special keys. My special keys could open many different doors. Perhaps I could open the stable doors with one of these keys.

I put one of the keys into the lock on the stable doors. I tried to turn the key, but it didn't turn. I put a different key into the lock. No luck! Then I heard a car coming towards the stables area. I didn't want anyone to see me near Stable 14. I put a third key into the lock. This time, the key turned! I opened the doors quickly and I stepped inside the stable. I locked the doors behind me.

There was very little light inside the stable. There was a smell of horses and straw. I looked around me. Along the wall to my left, there were stalls for horses. But there were no horses. All the stalls were empty. There were no stalls on the right-hand wall. And there were no doors and no windows in that wall. But there was a big cupboard on the wall, half-way along it. The cupboard was three metres high and two metres wide. There was

The cupboard was three metres high and two metres wide.

nothing in it – it was empty.

Then I heard a noise. The noise was very close to me. Was it coming from the big cupboard? No, the cupboard was empty. And there was nobody in the stable. I did not understand.

I opened the stable doors a little and I looked outside. I had a shock! The red 4x4 with the trailer had come back. It was reversing towards the stable doors. I closed the doors quickly and looked round again. Where could I hide? There was a pile of straw in the corner of the stable. I ran to the corner and hid myself under the straw.

I heard the stable doors open. Suddenly, there was more light inside the stable. Then I heard the car and the trailer coming in. I heard someone open the back of the trailer. I didn't move. I waited. I heard people moving in the stable.

After a few minutes, I heard someone shut the trailer. They opened the stable doors. The car and the trailer left the stable again and stopped outside. I heard someone shutting and locking the doors. The stable was darker again. Then I heard the car moving away. I was safe!

I lay under the straw and I waited. There was straw in my ears and in my nose. I waited and listened for a few minutes.

Then I got up and I walked towards the stable doors. I looked around. There was very little light and I almost fell over something. There was some more straw in the stable now, near the doors. And there was a bag of horse food.

'Someone is going to bring a horse here soon,' I thought. 'I must leave quickly.'

I unlocked the stable doors and opened them. I did not see anyone outside. I stepped out of the stable and turned round. I was going to lock the doors.

Suddenly, there was a terrible pain in my head. Someone had hit me on the head. Someone had hit me very hard. I fell to the ground.

A man's voice said, 'You were right, Dick. There *was* somebody hiding in the stable.'

Then someone put a bag over my head. And someone tied my hands behind my back with a rope.

I lay on the ground and waited. What next? There was a terrible pain in my stomach, then in my arms and then in my legs. Someone was kicking me very hard. Someone was kicking me again and again. Was I going to die?

Then another man spoke.

'Don't kill him! I want to ask him some questions!' he said.

The kicking stopped.

'OK, mister,' the second man said. 'What were you doing in the stable? Tell me! If you don't tell me, I'll kill you!'

I thought for a second. Someone kicked me again. This time, someone kicked my back. Was it Dick? Who *was* Dick? Dick Gates? Another kick!

'S—security,' I said. 'I'm a racecourse official. I'm checking security.'

A hand touched the yellow security pass.

'He *is* an official,' Dick said. 'What shall we do?'

'Leave him here,' the first voice said. 'He hasn't seen our faces.'

I heard the two men walk away. I lay on the ground. I could not see because the bag was over my head. I could not speak. I could not stand up. My hands were tied behind me. My whole body was painful. I fainted.

6
Back to L.A.

I woke up. I was lying on the ground. Where was I? I didn't know!

Then I remembered. I was in the stables area at Santa Rosita Racetrack. My hands were tied behind my back and there was a bag over my head! My whole body was painful.

What had happened to me? I remembered the two men. How long had I been on the ground? I tried to think.

Then I heard a voice. 'Who are you? What's happening here?'

I knew that voice! It was Slim.

I didn't reply. Slim took the bag off my head, then he quickly untied the rope. I moved my arms. I stood up slowly. It was dark now. I had been tied up for a long time.

'Lenny! Why are you tied up?' Slim asked.

I smiled. 'Hi, Slim,' I said. 'I was tired. I lay down here to sleep. While I was asleep, somebody tied me up. And they put this bag over my head!'

'Lenny, stop joking. I was worried about you. You didn't return the security pass,' said Slim. 'I've been looking for you for an hour. What happened?'

'I don't know,' I replied. 'Someone hit me on the head. They put a bag over my head and they tied my hands with a rope. They kicked me. I couldn't shout for help. I fainted!'

'Who did this, Lenny?' Slim asked. 'Who do you know at this racetrack?'

'I know you, Slim. But I don't know any other people here,' I said. 'And I don't know who did this to me.'

I didn't want to tell Slim about The Chief, or about the men in the red 4x4.

'Perhaps someone made a mistake,' I said. 'Please forget about this, Slim.'

'OK, someone made a mistake,' said Slim. 'They were trying to kill another person, not you!' Slim didn't believe my story. 'Come to my office and sit down for a few minutes,' he said.

I went with Slim to his office by the gateway. I sat in a chair while Slim made some coffee. He started to ask me some more questions. Suddenly, the phone rang. Slim answered the call. Then he put the phone down.

'Stay here and rest, Lenny,' he said. 'I have to go to the administrator's office for five minutes.'

Slim left the office. Quickly, I leant across his desk and opened the drawer. There were lots of yellow and blue passes in the drawer. I took a blue pass and I put it in my pocket. Then I closed the drawer.

Now I wanted to leave Santa Rosita as fast as possible. I left the yellow security pass on the desk and I walked to the car park.

I got into the Chrysler and I started the engine. I drove back to my office building and I parked the car. My whole body was painful. I had a terrible headache.

There was a red light on my telephone answering machine. There was a message for me. But I didn't listen to the message. I was tired. I looked at my watch. The time was 8.45 p.m. – dinner time! But I didn't want to eat anything. I wanted to sleep.

The phone rang. I didn't answer the phone. I didn't want to talk to anyone. I listened while the answering machine recorded another message.

'Hi, Lenny!' said the voice from the answering machine. 'This is Herman. I'm calling about my $1000. I'll see you tomorrow.'

Herman! I put my hand in my pocket. I had $200 which Sandy had given me. Would Herman be happy with $200? I didn't want to think about this problem.

I fell asleep.

―――

It was morning when I awoke. It was about 6.30 a.m. I didn't have a headache. But I was very tired. I got up and drank some water. Then I sat in my chair again.

'I'll sleep for another hour,' I said to myself.

Soon I was dreaming.

7

Sandy Again

I was dreaming about Hawaii again. The sun was shining on my face. The sound of the sea was around me. There was a beautiful woman standing next to me.

Suddenly, a hand was touching my arm. I opened my eyes. It was Sandy Bonner! She was standing beside me. Her hand was on my arm. My arm was painful.

'Ouch!' I said.

'Mr Samuel! Are you OK? Have you been in a fight?' she asked.

'I'm OK,' I said. I looked at my watch. It was 10.30 a.m. I looked at Sandy.

'I phoned you yesterday evening,' she said. 'You weren't here. But I left a message on your answering machine. Have you found The Chief?'

'No,' I said. 'But I'm learning a lot about horse racing. I want to ask you a question, Sandy. Who was your tall slim visitor yesterday?'

Suddenly, Sandy's face became pale. She was very frightened.

'I told you not to come to the ranch. They'll kill —' She stopped speaking.

'Who will they kill, Sandy?' I asked. 'Your tall slim friend tried to kill *me* yesterday.'

'*You?*' Sandy was surprised. 'Where did you meet him?'

'Forget about that,' I replied. 'Is there anything that you want to tell me? I must have some more information.'

'No, Mr Samuel,' said Sandy quietly. 'I can't tell you anything more.'

'Sandy,' I said. 'I want to help you. But you must help me. Tell me about Lou Weaver. Why does he walk around your ranch with a gun?'

'Lou is a good man,' she replied. 'He works for me. He takes care of the horses. He's worried about me. I can't tell you anything more!'

'Miss Bonner,' I said. 'Why won't you give me any information?'

'I can't tell you anything more,' Sandy said again. 'Now I must leave. If they see me here, they'll kill The Chief. I've paid you for the work that you did yesterday. But you made a mistake. I don't want you to do any more work for me. I won't come here again. And I won't phone you. Please forget about me and The Chief. And please stay away from the ranch!'

Sandy turned and she ran out of the room.

So, I wasn't working for Sandy Bonner any more. But I owed Herman money!

I took the $200 and the blue security pass from my pocket. I threw the pass into the waste bin. I put $50 back into my pocket and I put $150 in an envelope. I wrote Herman's name on the envelope. I left my office and I pushed the envelope under Herman's door. Then I drove home.

———

Two hours later, I was much better. At home, I had had a hot shower and some breakfast. And I had put on some clean clothes.

I decided to enjoy myself. I had only $50 but I decided to go to the races at Santa Rosita.

First, I drove back to my office. When I got to the office door, the phone was ringing. I picked up the phone.

35

'Hello,' I said. 'Lenny Samuel speaking.'

'Mr Samuel!' said a voice. It was Sandy Bonner. 'I'm sorry, Mr Samuel. I was wrong. A horse called Golden Dragon —'

Suddenly she stopped speaking.

'Sandy?' I said. 'What do you want to tell me?'

But there was no reply. I put the phone down.

I was going to Santa Rosita. But I wasn't working now. It was a lovely day and I was going to enjoy myself. I was going to forget about Sandy Bonner. I wasn't going to look for a horse called The Chief. And I wasn't going to ask about a horse called Golden Dragon. But I took the blue security pass from the waste bin. Then I opened the drawer of my desk and I took my gun from it. I put the pass and the gun in my pocket.

'Perhaps they'll be useful,' I said to myself. Then I left the office and I got into my car.

CD 2

8

Golden Dragon

The sun was shining as I drove to the Santa Rosita Racetrack. I was wearing my baseball cap and dark glasses again. My binoculars were in the car. In my pockets were the blue security pass, $50 and my gun.

I thought about Sandy. Why had she phoned me? And why had she stopped speaking suddenly? Why did she say the name, Golden Dragon? Where was The Chief now?

'Perhaps I'll look at Stable 14 again,' I said to myself. 'I'm not working for Sandy Bonner any more. But someone hit me outside Stable 14. Someone didn't want me to see inside it. Why not?'

I looked at the blue sky and the hot sun. It *was* a lovely day. I decided to watch a few races before I went to Stable 14.

The racetrack was very busy. It was Saturday and thousands of people had come to watch the races. The car-park was full of cars. I paid for my racetrack ticket. It cost $20. I paid for my car-park ticket. That cost $10. Now I had $20. I picked up my binoculars and I walked towards the track.

Many people were standing by the track. And many people were sitting in the grandstand. Everyone was watching the racing. I stood by the track and I watched three races. They were very exciting.

Many people bet on horses. They choose the horse which they want to win a race. They make a bet on it. They bet on the horse to win the race. They pay some money at a betting office. If the horse doesn't win the race, the betting office keeps their money. If the horse which they choose *is* the winner, the betting office gives them more money than they have paid.

There was a betting office at the racetrack. People who had come to watch the races could make their bets at this betting office. But there were also betting offices all over the country. People who were not at the racetrack could bet on the races at Santa Rosita too.

After each race, there was an announcement from the racetrack loudspeakers. This message told everyone which horse had won the race. People who had made bets on the winner were very happy!

A lot of people watched the races through binoculars.

I had brought my binoculars with me. But I didn't watch the horses through them. I watched the people. I was looking for a tall slim man.

Suddenly, I saw him. He was sitting in the grandstand. He was about thirty and he was wearing dark glasses and a dark suit. It was the man that I had seen at the ranch and in the red 4x4. He was talking to another man, who was sitting next to him. The other man was about ten years older. He was tall and heavy. He had long red hair, tied in a pony-tail. He was wearing a brown jacket. Sandy had told me about this man. It was Dick Gates!

I watched the two men through my binoculars. They couldn't see me. The men were talking and they were watching the races. The dark-haired man had a mobile phone and he was making lots of phone calls.

I moved the binoculars and I looked at some other people in the crowd. Suddenly, I saw another man that I knew – Herman!

Herman started to walk towards me. He was about one hundred metres away but he hadn't seen me. I didn't want to talk to Herman. But I wanted to watch the two other men, so I didn't move.

Herman came closer and closer. There were hundreds of people near the track, but Herman was big and tall. It was easy to see him! Now he was only twenty metres from me. I turned and started to walk quickly away from him.

I walked to the betting office. This was a long, low building with many windows. People were standing in lines at the windows. They were waiting to make their bets. Behind each window, there was a person who took people's money and wrote down the details of their bets. I joined a line.

'Perhaps Herman won't see me,' I thought.

Then a hand hit me on the back – a very large hand!

'Hi, Lenny!' Herman said loudly. 'What are you doing here? Do you like racing? I didn't know that.'

'Hi, Herman,' I replied quickly. 'Yes. I like racing. I want to bet on the next race.' I smiled at the huge bodyguard and pointed to the line of people at the betting window. Herman joined the line behind me.

'I want to talk to you about my money, Lenny,' Herman said. 'You made a mistake when you gave me the envelope. There was only $150 in it.'

'Oh! I'm sorry about that, Herman,' I said. The line of people was moving. I was getting nearer the betting window.

'Don't worry about it,' Herman said with a big smile.

'Give me my $850 now.'

I was almost at the front of the line. I was almost at the betting window. There was one man in front of me. I didn't know what to do.

'Herman —' I began.

'You're next, Lenny!' said Herman. He pushed me forward.

Suddenly, I was standing in front of the betting window. There was a woman behind it.

'Yes?' the woman said.

I took the money from my pocket. I had $20. And I had to bet on a horse quickly. I didn't know which one to choose. I looked at the list of horses for the next race. And I saw a name that I knew – Golden Dragon.

Golden Dragon was going to run in the next race. Only a few people were betting on the horse. His odds were 50-to-1.

'If Golden Dragon wins the race, I'll get fifty times more money than I bet on him,' I thought.

'I want to bet $20 on Golden Dragon to win the next race,' I said quickly.

The woman took my money. She gave me a piece of paper with the details of my bet written on it. I turned to Herman.

'I want to watch this race,' I said. 'After that, I'll give you your money.'

'OK, Lenny,' said Herman. 'Let's watch the race together.'

Herman bet on a horse called Margarita. Then we walked to the track. We waited for the race to start. I looked through my binoculars. Dick Gates and his friend were sitting in their seats. The thin dark man was speaking into his mobile phone again.

'Margarita is a winner, Lenny. Margarita is going to win this race,' Herman said. 'She won her last two races.'

'No, Golden Dragon will win,' I said.

Herman laughed. 'Golden Dragon!' he said. 'He's the slowest horse in the race. He's never won a race.'

The horses were going towards the starting gates.

Herman pointed to a big brown horse. His jockey was wearing a gold and black shirt. 'That's Golden Dragon,' he said. 'He won't win!'

'Golden Dragon is big and strong,' I said.

Herman looked at the horse again. 'Yes, you're right,' he said. 'He *is* big and strong. But he's a loser. Margarita is going to win.'

I looked at the horses through my binoculars. They were ready to start the race. Then I looked quickly at the grandstand. Dick Gates and his friend were holding binoculars. They were looking at the horses by the starting gates.

Suddenly, the crowd shouted. The starting gates had opened. The race had started! I looked at the horses galloping along the track. Golden Dragon was the slowest horse!

9

The Race

'Faster, Golden Dragon! Faster! *Faster!*'

Someone was shouting. It was me! The horses came round the track. They were galloping towards us. Margarita was in first place.

But Golden Dragon was in second place! At first, he had run slowly. But now he was running faster and faster!

The horses galloped past us. People were shouting. Golden Dragon and Margarita were side-by-side. The two horses crossed the finishing line together. Which horse had won? We waited while the officials looked at a photograph of the finish.

'That was amazing!' said Herman. 'Golden Dragon was very fast. He's never run so fast.'

Five minutes later, there was an announcement from the loudspeakers. 'The result of the last race is, first – Golden Dragon and second – Margarita.'

I jumped up and down and I put my arms round Herman.

'Wow!' Herman said. 'How much did you win?'

'Wait here,' I said. I walked to the betting window. I showed the woman the piece of paper with the details of my bet. She gave me my money. Golden Dragon had won at 50-to-1. And I had won $1000!

I gave Herman $850. Then I said goodbye to him.

I looked at the grandstand again. Where were Gates and his friend? They weren't sitting in their seats. Had they left after Golden Dragon's race? Perhaps they had bet on Golden Dragon too! But they hadn't left their seats before the race. I remembered the dark-haired man and the mobile phone. Perhaps they had been betting by phone. Yes! That was the answer.

But there were other questions. These two men knew Sandy. They had stolen The Chief. And Sandy had told me Golden Dragon's name. What was happening?

I walked away from the track. I took off my cap and my dark glasses. I walked towards the stables area. There were two security guards and some racetrack officials standing by the gateway to the stables area. Slim wasn't there.

I watched the gateway. The two guards stopped every car at the gateway. They checked the driver's ID. If there was a trailer, an official checked the horse's ID too.

I put the blue security pass round my neck and I walked up to the gate. I waved to the security guards and smiled. Then I walked through the gateway into the stables area.

The area was very busy. There were horses and cars and trailers everywhere. Jockeys in brightly-coloured clothes were talking to trainers. I walked slowly towards Stable 14.

I stopped about fifty metres from the large stable. I put on my cap and my dark glasses again and I stood near some trees. The red 4x4 and the trailer were parked outside Stable 14. I didn't see a horse in the trailer. I stood and I waited. Then someone that I knew walked towards Stable 14. It was Lou Weaver! I looked at his face. He was very pleased about something. But he was very worried about something too. He stood outside the stable.

A few minutes later, a jockey came towards Stable 14 with a big brown horse. The jockey was wearing a gold and black shirt. Lou spoke to the jockey and took the horse from him. I knew the horse. It was the winner of the last race – Golden Dragon!

I didn't understand. If Golden Dragon was Sandy Bonner's horse, why hadn't she told me this?

Then a man came out of the stable. It was the tall, dark-haired man. He held Lou's arm and they walked into the stable with the horse. The doors closed.

Ten minutes passed. Then the dark-haired man appeared again. He opened both of the stable doors and he reversed the red car and the trailer into the stable. He closed the doors behind him. I waited.

After another five minutes, the doors opened again and the 4x4 and the trailer came out. The dark-haired man was in the car. He stopped the car outside the stable, he got out and he went back inside the building.

I walked slowly towards the car and the trailer. Now there was a horse in the trailer. 'It's Golden Dragon,' I thought. 'He's going home after his race.'

I walked back towards the gateway. I sat on the ground by a tree. I had an idea. I was going to wait until the red car and the trailer left the racetrack. Then I was going to look inside Stable 14 again.

I had a lot of questions and I wanted some answers. I had been hit on the head and tied up with a rope outside this stable. Why had that happened? What were these two men doing? Why was Lou Weaver here? Did Sandy know about this?

I sat and waited. Ten minutes later, the red 4x4 and the trailer went past me and stopped at the gate. There were two people in the car now. One was the dark-haired man. I couldn't see the other person clearly. Was it Dick

The tall, dark-haired man held Lou's arm and they walked into Stable 14.

Gates? Or was it Lou Weaver?

The car and the horse were checked. Then the 4x4 went through the gateway and left the racetrack.

I was going to be careful today. I waited for an hour. The 4x4 did not come back. The stables area was not very busy now. And the sun was not so bright.

I took my special keys out of my pocket and I opened the doors of Stable 14. Soon, I was inside the building and I had closed the doors behind me.

It was dark inside the stable. I put my right hand on the wall. Was there a light switch? I moved my hand along the wall. Nothing! I moved forward slowly, with my hand on the wall.

At last, I found a switch. It was in a corner. I touched the switch. But no lights came on.

I was going to walk back to the doors. I was going to open the doors a little. I wanted some more light inside the stable. But I didn't move. I heard something. It was the noise of an electric motor. I took my gun out of my pocket.

Something very strange was happening. Light was coming into the dark stable. But it wasn't coming from outside. It was coming from the right-hand wall. After a few seconds, I could see clearly. The big cupboard was moving slowly! There was a door in the wall behind the cupboard. The cupboard was fixed to the door. The switch that I had touched had started an electric motor. And the electric motor was opening this secret door. Yes! The light was coming from behind the door!

The Chief

The light was coming from a room behind the secret door. In the room there was a stall. And in the stall there was a big brown horse.

I had heard a strange noise on my first visit to Stable 14. Now I understood. The noise had come from this room.

I walked towards the horse.

'Stand still!' a man's voice said. Something hard and

sharp was pushed into my back. I knew the voice. I started to turn towards the man.

'Stand still!' the man said again. 'Throw your gun behind you. Then lie down on the floor.'

I did what the man told me to do. I lay on the floor and I waited for a few seconds. Then I turned over very quickly. Lou Weaver was standing beside me. He was holding a large fork. It was a fork that was used for moving straw. Very quickly, I pulled the fork from Lou's hands and I kicked his legs. I kicked them very hard. Lou gave a loud cry and he fell down on the floor beside me.

I picked up my gun and I moved over to Lou. I sat on his chest. The old man couldn't move. And I had the gun.

'OK, Lou,' I said. 'Do you remember me?'

'Yes, I remember you,' Lou replied. 'You came to the ranch yesterday.' Then he looked at my security pass. 'Are you an official here?' he asked. He was frightened.

'No,' I said. 'My name's Lenny Samuel. I'm a private detective. I'm working for Sandy Bonner. I'm looking for The Chief.'

I showed Lou my detective's licence. He was surprised.

'OK,' he said. 'You've found The Chief. But Sandy knows where he is.'

'What do you mean?' I asked.

'Let me get up and I'll tell you everything,' Lou said.

We stood up. Lou walked over to the stall and pointed to the big brown horse.

'This is The Chief,' he said. 'I'm taking care of him here until tomorrow.'

'Why is The Chief here at the racetrack?' I asked. 'And why is he in this secret room?'

Lou touched the horse's nose. The Chief made a soft noise.

'Golden Dragon didn't run in the last race,' Lou said. 'The Chief ran in the race. The officials didn't know about it. The Chief and Golden Dragon are the same height and the same colour. But The Chief runs much faster than Golden Dragon. He's a winner!'

'But the racetrack officials check the horses' passports and tattoos on racing days,' I said. 'The Chief's ID and Golden Dragon's IDs are different.'

'Yes. The officials check the horses' IDs on racing days,' Lou said. 'They check the IDs when the horses arrive and they check them again when they leave. But nobody checks them on training days. The Chief came here in the trailer yesterday afternoon. He was put in this secret room. The trailer was empty when it left the racetrack. Nobody checked the trailer. The Chief stayed here last night.

'This morning,' Lou went on, 'Golden Dragon came here in the trailer. The officials checked his passport and his tattoo. But Golden Dragon didn't run in the race. This afternoon, Golden Dragon was put in this secret room. The Chief was taken to the track. The Chief ran in the race instead of Golden Dragon. The Chief won the race. Then he was brought to this room again. And Golden Dragon was taken away in the trailer. His ID was checked at the gate.

'The Chief will stay in this room again tonight,' Lou continued. 'There is no racing tomorrow. Sundays are training days. When the trailer comes tomorrow, it will be empty. Nobody will check it. Then The Chief will go back to the ranch.'

50

'So you are working *with* these criminals,' I said. 'And Sandy knew about it. You are criminals too! How much money did you and Sandy win, Lou?'

'Miss Bonner and I haven't won anything!' Lou said angrily. 'Gates and his friend, Ventanas, are the criminals. They own Golden Dragon. They came to our ranch on Thursday morning and Gates stole The Chief. We didn't know their plan then. At midday today, they came to the ranch again. They told us about their plan. They put Sandy in a storeroom and they locked the door. They had guns. They made me come here with them. Ventanas said, "If you don't help us look after The Chief, we'll kill Sandy Bonner." I *had* to help them.'

Suddenly, there was a noise from the front of the stable. Lou pulled the gun out of my hand.

'Be quiet!' he said. 'Stay here with the horse and don't make a noise. Gates and Ventanas have come back. If they find you here, they'll kill you.'

I lay down in the straw next to The Chief. He was very big. 'Please don't stand on me,' I whispered to him.

'Weaver!' a man's voice shouted. 'Where are you? Why is that door open?'

Lou walked towards the front of the stable. I could not see anything. But I could hear the conversation.

'I'm sorry, Mr Gates,' Lou said. 'I was hot. And The Chief was hot after the race and —'

'Forget about the horse!' Gates shouted. 'The horse will be dead tomorrow.'

'Dead? Why?' Lou Weaver asked angrily. 'We've done everything that you wanted. The Chief ran in the race instead of Golden Dragon. The Chief won the race for you. Now you must let Sandy go free. You must go away

51

and never come back!'

The other man – Ventanas – laughed. It was a cruel laugh.

'We won $5 million when Golden Dragon won the race,' he said. 'We made bets all over the country. We made our bets by phone. We don't want anyone to find out about that. So The Chief will die. And we'll kill the girl and we'll kill you too, Weaver.'

'Kill Sandy?' Lou said angrily. 'No!'

There was a loud bang and a cry of pain.

There were two more loud bangs and then there was another noise. Something fell to the ground.

'I've shot him, Dick,' Ventanas said. 'Are you OK?'

'No!' Gates said. 'The stupid old man has shot me in the arm.'

Very carefully, I looked out from The Chief's stall. Lou Weaver was lying on the ground. My gun was on the ground beside him. Ventanas was holding a gun. Dick Gates was holding his right arm with his left hand. There was blood on his hand.

'What shall I do with the horse?' Ventanas asked. 'Shall I kill it?' He picked up my gun. Then he started to walk towards The Chief and me.

'No,' Gates said. 'We'll leave it here and lock the doors. The horse will die.'

'OK, Dick,' said Ventanas. 'Where are we going now?'

'We're going to the Ride-A-Winner Ranch,' Gates said. 'We're going to kill Sandy Bonner. Then no one will know about our plan.'

I heard the stable doors close. I heard the key turn in the lock. Gates and his friend were going to kill Sandy. I had to move fast.

Lou Weaver was lying on the ground.

11

L.A. Winners

When Gates and Ventanas had left, I came out of the
secret stall. Lou Weaver was badly hurt, but he was alive.
There was a bullet in his shoulder. His shoulder was
bleeding. There was a lot of blood.

I took off Lou's shirt and tore a piece of cloth from it. I
tied the cloth round his shoulder. I covered the hole in
his shoulder. But I couldn't stay with him. I had to get to
the Ride-A-Winner Ranch. I had to get there quickly.
Gates and his friend had driven away fifteen minutes
before. And they were going to kill Sandy!

'Someone will come and take care of you, Lou,' I said.
'You're going to be OK!'

Then I thought of something. The races had finished
now. People were leaving the racetrack and going home.
There was going to be a lot of traffic. The roads were
going to be full of cars. The Ride-A-Winner Ranch was
only a few kilometres away. But I couldn't drive there in
less than an hour. What could I do?

Suddenly, something pushed me in the back. What
was it? Was it a gun? I turned round quickly. It was The
Chief. He had come out of his stall. He was looking for
Lou. The big horse saw the old man lying on the ground.
The Chief went to him and touched Lou's body with his
mouth. The horse was trying to help his old friend.

Then, I had a plan. I looked around the stable. There
was a piece of rope hanging on the wall. I tied the rope
around The Chief's head and neck. I whispered to the
horse.

'Come with me, Chief. We're going to help Sandy.'

I took the horse towards the stable doors. Gates and Ventanas had locked them. I took the special keys from my pocket.

A minute later, The Chief and I were outside the stable. I left the doors open.

It was late afternoon. I looked around. People were putting horses in trailers. No one was watching us. I had to hurry. Soon it was going to be dark.

'OK,' I said to The Chief. 'I've never ridden a horse before. It's going to be difficult. But I have to try.'

I jumped onto The Chief and we moved towards the gateway. I looked ahead. Slim and another security guard were standing at the gate. Some racetrack officials were with them. They were checking IDs. A car with a trailer was going through the gateway.

I kicked my feet on The Chief's sides. We galloped towards the gate. Suddenly, Slim saw us. He tried to shut the gate.

'Stop!' Slim shouted. 'What are you doing? Where are you going?'

I didn't reply. Slim stood in the gateway for a moment, then he ran. The Chief galloped through the gateway. I turned the horse in the car park and we stopped.

I shouted to Slim.

'There's a man in Stable 14. He's been shot!' I shouted. 'Call a doctor. And call the police!'

Then I turned The Chief again and we galloped across the car park.

There were long lines of cars leaving the racetrack. But we weren't going to go on the road. We were going to gallop across the fields towards the ranch.

'There's a man in Stable 14. He's been shot!' I shouted.
'Call a doctor. And call the police!'

I held on tightly to the rope round The Chief's neck. The big brown horse galloped very fast. He knew where his home was. I smiled. Riding was easy!

But then I saw a fence in front of us. Galloping was not difficult. But could we jump the fence? I kicked my feet on the horse's sides and The Chief jumped. He went over the fence but I did not stay with him. Crash! I fell onto the dusty ground.

I sat on the ground. My shoulder was painful. And I was worried. How could I get to the ranch now?

Then I heard a noise. It was the horse. The Chief was walking back to me. He came up to me and waited. I stood up slowly. I jumped onto The Chief's back. We started galloping again.

I saw the ranch in the distance. There was a car moving along the track to the white ranch house. It was a red 4x4. Were we too late?

As we got closer to the ranch, we slowed down. Soon, The Chief was walking quietly. The big brown horse was tired. He had worked hard that day.

The red 4x4 had stopped in front of the white ranch house. The Chief and I went to the side of the house and I watched the door. After a minute, the door opened and Dick Gates and Sandy Bonner came out. Gates was pushing Sandy in front of him. He had a gun in his left hand. Sandy's hands were tied with a rope. And Ventanas was walking behind Gates and Sandy. He had a gun too.

Suddenly, Sandy stopped walking. She turned and looked at Gates.

'Where's Lou?' she shouted at him.

'He's dead,' Gates replied. 'The stupid old man shot me.' Gates pointed to the blood on his right arm.

Sandy started to cry. 'Please leave me,' she said. 'I won't tell anyone about you. You took The Chief and you won your money. Now you've killed a kind old man. Please go and leave me.'

'Be quiet and get into the car!' Gates shouted. He pointed the gun at Sandy.

No one had seen The Chief and me. We were standing quietly at the side of the house.

'Get into the car!' Gates shouted again.

I kicked The Chief. The horse and I moved forward. The two criminals heard the horse and they turned round. But we were only five metres away.

'Go! Chief, go!' I shouted.

The horse jumped at the red-haired man and hit him very hard. Gates fell to the ground. There was a shot. The shot came from Gates' gun. Ventanas cried with pain and fell to the ground too. Gates had shot him!

I jumped down from the horse. I ran back to Sandy. She was looking down at Ventanas.

'He's OK,' she said. 'When The Chief hit Gates, Gates shot his friend in the leg.'

Gates was lying on the ground. He was not moving. His eyes were closed.

I picked up the two guns. Then I untied the rope from Sandy's hands and I tied it round the criminals' hands. I took the mobile phone from Ventanas' pocket. Quickly, I called the police.

After that, I told Sandy about my visits to the Santa Rosita Racetrack. I told her about the secret room in Stable 14. And I told her about Lou Weaver and my ride from the racetrack.

'Lou isn't dead,' I said.

58

The horse jumped at the red-haired man.

'I couldn't tell you about Gates and Ventanas this morning. I was frightened,' Sandy said. 'But I was worried about Lou. He's a good man. Will he be OK?'

'Yes, Lou will be OK,' I said. 'What happened here? Tell me the whole story now.'

'I told you the truth when I came to see you yesterday morning,' Sandy said. 'Gates came here on Thursday morning and he took The Chief.

'On Thursday afternoon,' Sandy went on, 'I had a phone call from Ventanas. I told you about that. He said, "I've got The Chief. I've borrowed him. I'll return him after a few of days. But if you tell the police, I'll kill the horse. We're watching you." I believed him, Mr Samuel,' said Sandy.

'Yesterday morning, I didn't know any more facts,' Sandy went on. 'Gates and Ventanas hadn't phoned me again. They hadn't asked for money for The Chief. Lou and I didn't know what to do. So, I thought about a private detective. I saw your name and address in the phone book and I came to your office. Lou didn't know about my plan. But Ventanas came to the ranch on Friday afternoon. He asked me about The Chief and about Lou. He wanted me to help him. But he didn't tell me his plan. He frightened me. I hit him. He was very angry.

'This morning, I went to Los Angeles and spoke to you again,' Sandy went on. 'I said, "Forget about me and The Chief." But when I got back here, Gates and Ventanas were here again. They told us their plan. They wanted to take Lou to the racetrack. The Chief was behaving badly. They wanted Lou to take care of him. Ventanas had a gun. He was going to kill Lou if he didn't go with them.

'So,' Sandy said, 'I phoned you. I phoned you while

Ventanas and Gates were taking Lou to their car. I tried to tell you about their plan. But Gates came back into the house. He heard me speaking to you and I couldn't tell you everything. Gates locked me in a storeroom.'

'They were going to kill me this evening,' Sandy said. 'Thank you for saving me. Thank you for everything, Mr Samuel.'

'I was pleased to help you,' I replied. 'But it was The Chief who saved you!'

Sandy put her arms round the horse's neck. 'He's wonderful,' she said and she smiled. I wanted her to put her arms round *my* neck. But she liked the horse, not me!

'Come to the ranch any time, Mr Samuel,' Sandy said. 'Come and ride The Chief again. He likes you!'

'That's very kind of you,' I said. 'But I won't ride again. I'd never ridden a horse before today. And today I rode a winner! But it was too exciting. Being a private detective and catching criminals is less dangerous!'

Points for Understanding

1

1 It was a Friday morning. Lenny was asleep in his office.
   (a)   Why was he asleep?
   (b)   Who woke him?
2 When Lenny said, 'I'm the best private detective in L.A.',
   his visitor laughed. Why did the visitor laugh?

2

1 Who was Herman?
2 Was Lenny pleased to see him? Why/why not?
3 Lenny's visitor walked to the window and looked down into
   the street. What was the reason for this?

3

1 Lenny looked through his binoculars and he saw two people
   inside the ranch house.
   (a)   Who were they?
   (b)   What happened next?
2 Who was Lou Weaver? Why didn't he believe Lenny's story?

4

1 Slim was in his office but he saw Lenny entering the stables
   area. How?
2 Slim could not give Lenny a blue pass. Why not?

5

1 How did Lenny get into Stable 14?
2 Lenny heard a noise in Stable 14 but he did not know where

it was coming from. There is a sentence which gives the reader a clue about the noise. Which sentence is it?

6

1 Why didn't Lenny tell Slim about the men in the red 4x4?
2 Why did Lenny take a blue pass from Slim's desk?

7

Sandy told Lenny, 'You made a mistake.' What was Lenny's mistake?

8

1 At the racetrack, Lenny saw Herman again. Was he pleased to see him? Why/why not?
2 Golden Dragon's odds were 50-to-1. What does this mean?

9

1 How had Lenny won $1000?
2 Lou Weaver took Golden Dragon from his jockey. Lenny didn't understand what was happening. Why not?

10

1 Lou Weaver saw Lenny's security pass and he was frightened. Why?
2 'I *had* to help them,' Lou Weaver said. Why did he have to help Gates and his friend?

11

1 Why was Lenny galloping across the fields, not along the road?
2 Who was Ventanas?

Exercises

People in the Story

Write the correct name next to each description below.

Dick Gates   Herman
The Chief   Sandy Bonner
Lou Weaver   Slim Peters
Ventanas   ~~Lenny Samuel~~

	Name	Description
1	*Lenny Samuel*	male; age mid-thirties; untidy appearance; a private detective
2		male; age about thirty; tall and heavy; works as a bodyguard for film stars
3		female; age twenty-five; has long dark hair; owns a ranch and keeps horses
4		male; age about sixty; employed as a ranch hand
5		male; age mid-forties; big man, quite fat; employed as a racetrack security guard
6		male; age about forty; tall and heavy; has long red hair which he ties in a pony-tail;
7		male; age about thirty; tall slim man with dark hair; owns a racehorse called Golden Dragon
8		male; age twelve; two metres high; has brown hair and brown eyes; retired from his former job

Words From the Story 1

Write the words from the box next to the correct meaning below.

describe   security pass   straw   borrow   gallop   jockey
smog   4x4 (four-by-four)   retire   stall   ranch   stable
detective   trailer   official   odds   racetrack
security guard   bet   racehorse

	Word	Meaning
1	describe	to say what something or someone looks like or what happened
2	borrow	to take and use something that you will give back after a short time to the *lender*
3	detective	a person whose job is to find out who committed a crime
4	smog	a mixture of smoke and fog – a form of pollution
5	trailer	a vehicle for carrying a horse
6	4x4 four by	a four-wheel-drive car: the engine turns all four wheels
7	racehours	a horse used for racing against other horses
8	racetrack	a circular path for racing horses
9	security guard	a man who works for a security company and guards a place
10	retire	to stop working because you are too old
11	bet	to gamble money on who will win a race etc
12	odds	the rate at which money is bet on a race
13	official	a person who is officially working for an organisation or is responsible to a committee
14	security pass	a card that allows you to go into a restricted area
15	stable	a place for housing horses
16	gallop	to run very quickly – used for horses not people
17	jokey	a man who rides a horse in a horse race
18	ranch	an American farm for animals, especially cattle and horses
19	straw	dried grass put on the floor of a stable and fed to horses
20	stall	the partition in a stable where a horse is kept

Words From the Story 2

Complete the sentences using words from the box on page 65 in the correct form.

1 Sandy Bonner wanted to find The Chief, so she hired a private
   detective .

2 Lenny Samuel wanted to know what the horse looked like. He
   asked Sandy Bonner to .... the horse.

3 Lenny had .... $1000 from
   Herman but he could not pay the money back.

4 Sandy Bonner kept horses on a ....
   called RIDE-A-WINNER.

5 Los Angeles has a pollution problem. You cannot see across the city
   because the air is clouded with ....

6 A kind of car which is good for driving off-road is a ....

7 The Chief and Golden Dragon are ....

8 Lenny visited the .... at Santa Rosita.

9 Lenny's old friend Slim Peters worked at Santa Rosita as a
   ....

10 The Chief stopped racing when he was twelve years old. He
   '...'

11 Ventanas took Golden Dragon to the racetrack in a closed
   ....

12 Golden Dragon and The Chief were kept in .... 14.

13 Lenny needed a .... to
   get to the stables, because the stables were in a restricted area.

14 Lenny took a blue pass from Slim's office and pretended to be a racecourse ....

15 The best racehorse riders are small men. Horses can run faster if their .... do not weigh much.

16 Golden Dragon was kept in a .... in the stable, but The Chief was hidden in a secret room at the side of the stable.

17 Lenny .... $20 on Golden Dragon to win.

18 The .... on Lenny's $20 bet were 50-to-1 so he received $1000 when Golden Dragon won the race.

19 Lenny hid under a pile of .... in the stable.

20 Lenny rode on The Chief and .... back to the ranch. The horse ran very fast.

Word Focus 1: *borrow* and *lend*

borrow = to take and use something that you will give back after a short time.

lend = to give someone something for a short time, expecting that they will give it back to you later.

Lenny borrowed $1000 from Herman. Lenny was the borrower. Herman was the lender.

Rewrite the sentences using the word in brackets (*lend/borrow*). Then complete the gaps.

1	Ron borrowed $1000 from the bank.
(lend)	*The Bank lent Ron $1000.*
Lender:	*The Bank*
Borrower:	*Ron*

2
(lend)

Kate borrowed six books from the library.

Lender: ....

....

Borrower: ....

3
(borrow)

Ellie lent Michael her ruler.

Lender: ....

....

Borrower: ....

4
(borrow)

Margaret's mother lent her a coat.

Lender: ....

....

Borrower: ....

Word Focus 2: *win* and *lose*

Write sentences using the words in brackets (*win/lose*).

1

Liverpool scored two goals and Arsenal scored one goal in the football match.

(win) *Liverpool won the football match.*

(lose) *Arsenal lost the football match.*

2

The result of the basketball game was Celtics 42 and Dolphins 27.

(win) ....

(lose) ....

3

In the election, Governor Shrub received 40% of the votes and Senator Cloony 60%.

(win) ....

(lose) ....

4

In the boat race between Oxford and Cambridge Universities, Cambridge crossed the finishing line first.

(win) ....

(lose) ....

Multiple Choice

Tick the correct meaning for each sentence.

1 'Nobody wanted to hire me.' (page 5)
a ☐ Nobody wanted to make me feel taller.
b ☐ Nobody wanted to rent my car.
c ☑ There was no work for me.
d ☐ Somebody wanted to fire me.

2 'Perhaps this woman is a client.' (page 5)
a ☐ This lady may be looking for a job.
b ☐ This lady may want to have some work done.
c ☐ This lady definitely wants to work for someone.
d ☐ This lady may be a businesswoman.

3 'I'm in the wrong business.' (page 11)
a ☐ I haven't understood what I'm being told.
b ☐ I'm asking the wrong questions.
c ☐ I'm doing the wrong job.
d ☐ I've gone the wrong way.

4 'There was no racing today. These horses were training.' (page 19)
a ☐ These horses were going on a train to a race tomorrow.
b ☐ These horses were not racehorses.
c ☐ When there was no racing, the horses were kept in the stables.
d ☐ These horses were exercising because there were no races.

5 'Some retired racehorses are used for breeding.' (page 24)
a ☐ Some racehorses go to shows when they finish racing.
b ☐ Some horses that don't race any more become parents to young horses.
c ☐ Some old racehorses are used as dog meat.
d ☐ When racehorses stop racing they often help to train others.

6 'The officials check the horses' ID on racing days.' (page 50)

a ☐ When there are races, people who work at the racecourse check the horses' identity.

b ☐ People who work at the racecourse make sure the horses are healthy after races.

c ☐ The horses' owners make sure they are fit before races.

d ☐ The horses are given special names before races.

Story Outline

Read the story outline. Then answer the questions.

Sandy Bonner comes to Lenny's office. There is a notice on the door: L. SAMUEL – PRIVATE INVESTIGATOR.

Sandy tells Lenny about The Chief, her racehorse. The horse has disappeared.

Lenny wants $200 a day to find the horse. He owes Herman, from the office next door, $1000, and he has no money. He needs a job.

A bad man has taken The Chief. The man's name is Ventanas. He owns a racehorse called Golden Dragon. But Golden Dragon has never won a race. The Chief, however, was one of the best racehorses before it retired.

Ventanas puts The Chief in a race. But he says that The Chief is Golden Dragon. The betting shops give good odds on Golden Dragon because the horse has never won a race. They give odds of 50-to-1. The Chief/Golden Dragon wins the race, so Ventanas will be very rich. He bet $100,000 dollars on Golden Dragon.

Lenny only has $20. He bets on Golden Dragon and wins $1000. He pays Herman back.

After the race, Ventanas plans to kill Sandy and The Chief. He will have $5 million and no one will know his secret.

Lenny saves The Chief. He rides the horse from the racetrack to Sandy's ranch. He stops Ventanas before he can kill Sandy. He calls the police. Ventanas is arrested. The ending is happy for the L. A. Winners.

And if Golden Dargon wins
Vant a

1 What was Lenny Samuel's job?

....

2 What kind of a horse was The Chief?

....

3 How much money did Lenny want, per day, to find The Chief?

....

4 Who had lent $1000 to Lenny?

....

5 Who had taken The Chief?

....

6 How many races had Golden Dragon won?

....

7 Which horse ran in the race, The Chief or Golden Dragon?

....

8 What did Lenny do with the $1000 he won?

....

9 What did Ventanas plan to do after the race?

....

10 How much did Ventanas win when Golden Dragon/The Chief
   won the race?

....

11 What happened to Ventanas?

....

12 Does the story have a sad ending?

....

Published by Macmillan Heinemann ELT
Between Towns Road, Oxford OX4 3PP
Macmillan Heinemann ELT is an imprint of
Macmillan Publishers Limited
Companies and representatives throughout the world
Heinemann is a registered trademark of Harcourt Education, used under licence.

ISBN 978 0 2300 3510 2
ISBN 978 1 4050 7697 5 (with CD pack)

Text © Philip Prowse 1998, 2002, 2005
First published 1998

Design and illustration © Macmillan Publishers Limited 2002, 2005

This edition first published 2005

Designed by Sue Vaudin
Illustrated by Bob Harvey
Original cover template design by Jackie Hill
Cover illustration by Mark Oldroyd

ovf 11 9∧ ſε19

Printed in Thailand
2010 2009 2008
5 4 3 2 1

with CD pack
2010 2009 2008
9 8 7 6 5